My Secret Unicorn

A Special Friend

Linda Chapman

Illustrated by Biz Hull

PUFFIN

PUFFIN BOOKS

UK | USA | Canada | Ireland | Australia
India | New Zealand | South Africa

Puffin Books is part of the Penguin Random House group of companies
whose addresses can be found at global.penguinrandomhouse.com.

www.penguin.co.uk   www.puffin.co.uk   www.ladybird.co.uk

First published 2003
This edition published 2018

001

Written by Linda Chapman
Text copyright © Working Partners Ltd, 2003
Illustrations copyright © Biz Hull, 2003
Created by Working Partners Ltd, London W6 0QT

The moral right of the author and illustrator has been asserted

Typeset in 14.25/21.5 pt Bembo
Printed in Great Britain by Clays Ltd, St Ives plc

A CIP catalogue record for this book is available from the British Library

ISBN: 978-0-241-35423-0

All correspondence to:
Puffin Books
Penguin Random House Children's
80 Strand, London WC2R ORL

To Michelle Misra – for making
My Secret Unicorn so magical

CHAPTER

One

'Lauren! Are you ready? The Parkers are here!' Mrs Foster said, looking out of the kitchen window.

Lauren fed the remains of her toast to Buddy, her brother Max's young Bernese mountain dog. He gobbled up the crusts with a gulp and then bounded round in front of her.

'Out of the way, Buddy!' Lauren said,

laughing. She grabbed her riding hat
from the table. 'See you later, Mum.'

'Have fun!' Mrs Foster called.

'I will.' Lauren hurried out of the house to the car. Her friend Jessica sat in the back with her stepsister, Samantha. They were going to be choosing a pony and Lauren was helping them!

'Hello, Lauren,' Mr Parker said, smiling at her as she got into the back of the car.

'Hi,' Lauren said. She exchanged grins with Jessica and Samantha. They were both looking very excited.

Mr Parker started the engine. 'OK, everyone. High Meadows farm, here we come.'

The stables were a fifteen-minute drive from Lauren's house on the outskirts of town. A signpost at the top of the farm's drive read:

> ## High Meadows
> ## – riding school and pony sales
> ## Proprietor: T. Bradshaw

At the end of the drive were two red barns, an office and a large training ring.

As Mr Parker stopped the car, a woman with curly auburn hair came out of the office. 'Hi there,' she said, smiling as they piled out of the car. 'You must be the Parkers?'

Mr Parker nodded. 'Yes, this is Samantha and Jessica and Jessica's friend, Lauren.'

'I'm Tina Bradshaw,' the woman said. She glanced at Jessica and Samantha. 'So, you're looking for a pony?'

They both nodded.

Tina smiled. 'Then come with me – I have plenty for you to see.'

She led the way across the yard and into the first barn. On either side of the wide central aisle ponies peered over half doors, their ears pricked.

'I'll show you the ponies I think might be most suitable and then you can choose three or four you'd like to try out in the ring,' Tina said. She headed over to a stall where a chestnut with a white blaze was looking out. 'This is Puzzle. He's ten years old and a very good jumper.

Next to him is …'

Lauren's brain was soon spinning with
pony names. After looking at twelve
ponies in the barn, Samantha and Jessica
had chosen four to ride – Bullfinch,
Puzzle, Lacey and Sandy. Tina saddled
them and led them to the training ring.

'Why don't you try Puzzle first?' she

said to Jessica,

handing her

the reins of

the chestnut. 'And Samantha, you try Bullfinch.'

Lauren watched as Samantha and Jessica took turns to ride the ponies around the ring. All of them looked lovely and she didn't know which one she'd choose if it were up to her.

Seeing some ponies looking over the gate of a field a little way off, Lauren wandered over to see them. There was a palomino – tan-coloured with a pale gold mane and tail – a bay and a black. Lauren stroked them and then she noticed another pony – a shaggy little dapple-grey – standing all by herself further up the field.

Lauren stared. The dapple-grey was exactly like her pony, Twilight! Although Twilight looked like an ordinary pony, he had an exciting secret. At certain times of the day, Lauren could say the words of the Turning Spell, which transformed Twilight into a unicorn!

Lauren hurried round the fence. As she

got closer she saw that the dapple-grey pony was a bit smaller and scruffier than Twilight, but otherwise just like him. She even had the same pattern of dapples on her coat.

Lauren picked a handful of long grass. 'Here,' she called, holding the grass out. 'Here, girl.'

The grey mare lifted her head slightly.

'Come on,' Lauren encouraged.

The mare walked over. Stopping by the fence, she reached out and took the grass, her soft grey lips nuzzling Lauren's palm.

On her head-collar was a brass name-plate. 'Moonshine,' Lauren read out. 'Is that your name?'

The pony
looked at her
with sad dark
eyes and a
memory stirred
in Lauren's mind.
The very first time she had
seen Twilight he had looked at
her in exactly the same way. It was so
weird. He and this pony were so alike
they might almost be brother and sister. A
thought struck Lauren and she almost
gasped out loud. No, she couldn't be
right ...

'Moonshine, are ... are you a unicorn
in disguise, just like Twilight?' she
whispered.

CHAPTER
Two

Moonshine stared at Lauren. 'I know about unicorns,' Lauren said quickly. 'I have one myself.'

'Lauren!' Hearing Jessica, Lauren turned.

'Come and tell me which pony you like best,' Jessica called to her.

Lauren didn't want to leave Moonshine. 'Just a minute,' she replied.

She looked at the little grey pony again. 'I won't tell anyone,' she whispered. 'Please – are you a unicorn?'

Moonshine didn't move.

'Lauren!' Jessica called impatiently.

Lauren gave up on getting Moonshine to respond. 'Coming!' She hurried back to the ring, her thoughts racing.

Jessica was riding Sandy around the ring for a second time. Seeing Lauren coming over, she called out, 'Watch how Sandy goes and then you can tell me which pony you like best.'

Lauren nodded and went to stand by Tina at the gate.

Tina smiled at her. 'I saw you talking to Moonshine just now.'

'She's lovely,' Lauren said.

Tina nodded. 'I think so too, but no
one ever wants to buy her. I guess she
doesn't look flashy enough. It's a shame,
she's got a heart of gold. You're not
looking for a pony, are you?'

Lauren shook her head regretfully. She
would have loved to buy Moonshine but

she knew her parents would never agree.

'Pity,' Tina sighed. 'Moonshine could do with some love. The girls who help out here prefer riding the livelier ponies and she doesn't get much attention. Oh, well.' She turned away to speak to Mr Parker.

Jessica rode over. 'So, which do you like best?' she asked eagerly.

'I like them all,' Lauren said truthfully. She watched the palomino Jessica was riding. 'Sandy's very pretty.'

'She's my favourite,' Jessica confided. 'But I think Sam likes Bullfinch.' She looked curiously at Tina. 'What were you and Tina talking about?'

'About that pony over there,' Lauren

said, pointing to Moonshine who was still standing by the fence in the field.

Jessica stared. 'Isn't she sweet? She looks just like Twilight!'

Lauren nodded.

'I'll ask if we can try her out,' Jessica said.

Lauren felt a leap of excitement. If Moonshine was a unicorn and Jessica bought her, it would be brilliant! But to Lauren's disappointment, when Jessica asked, Tina shook her head.

'Moonshine will be too small for Samantha,' she told Jessica. 'She's only 12.2 hands high. You need a pony who's at least 13.2.'

'Oh,' Jessica said, looking at Lauren.

'OK, Samantha,' Mr Parker called.
'Come over here. It's decision time.'

Samantha rode over on Bullfinch.

'So which pony is it to be?' Mr Parker
asked her and Jessica.

'Sandy,' Jessica said immediately.

'Bullfinch,' said Samantha at the same
moment.

'Not Bullfinch,' Jessica put in quickly. 'He's too heavy and slow.'

'He's obedient and reliable,' Samantha said, patting the buckskin's neck. 'Not like Sandy. She refused when I tried to jump her.'

'She didn't with me,' Jessica said.

'Fluke,' Samantha said.

'It *wasn't*!' Jessica declared hotly.

'Sandy's only young,' Tina said. 'She's still learning about jumping, so she might stop a little more than an experienced pony. But once she gets used to jumps she should be just fine.'

'Well, I want Bullfinch,' Samantha announced.

'And I want Sandy!' Jessica frowned.

Mr Parker looked at Tina. 'I'm sorry about this — there seems to be some disagreement.'

'That's OK,' Tina said understandingly. 'Buying a pony is a big commitment. You have to be sure you're getting the right one. How about you talk it over tonight and come back tomorrow? You can try them both out again then.'

Mr Parker looked relieved. 'Are you sure that would be OK?'

Tina nodded. 'No problem.'

As soon as Lauren got home she raced to Twilight's field and told him all about Moonshine.

'So, what do you think?' she demanded

eagerly. 'Do you think she might be a unicorn?'

Twilight stamped a hoof. Lauren wished she could turn him into a unicorn so that they could speak properly, but she knew her dad was working nearby so she couldn't risk it.

'We'll talk about it tonight, when it starts
to get dark,' she promised.

It was nearly twilight and Lauren went
back to the house. She fetched a can of
lemonade from the fridge and went up to
her bedroom. This was her favourite
place in the whole house. It had a sloping
ceiling, and a large window with a
window seat which looked down on to
Twilight's paddock. Lauren looked out.
Twilight was grazing in the shade of the
trees. He looked happy. She blew him a
kiss before picking up an old blue book
that was lying on the window seat. It was
called *The Life of a Unicorn* and it had
been given to her by Mrs Fontana, an old
lady who owned a bookshop. Mrs

Fontana was the only person in the world who knew about Twilight.

Sitting down, Lauren curled her legs underneath her and carefully opened up the book. After Twilight, it was one of her most treasured possessions. In the back of it were the words of the Turning Spell.

Lauren leafed carefully through the book, her eyes scanning the yellowing, faded pages. At last, she found what she was looking for. A picture of a little grey pony. It was a unicorn in its pony form.

She turned back a page and read the
words ...

Descendants of the two young unicorns that
Noah took on to the Ark still roam the Earth
today. They look like small ponies. Each of
them hopes to find someone who will learn
how to free them from their mortal form.

Lauren turned again to the picture of the
small grey pony. Both Twilight and
Moonshine were just like it. Lauren
stared out of the window, frowning
slightly. Was Moonshine a unicorn? She
and Twilight had to find out!

As soon as she could that evening, Lauren

rushed out to find Twilight. Quickly she said the words of the Turning Spell that changed him into a unicorn:

Twilight Star, Twilight Star,
Twinkling high above so far.
Shining light, shining bright,
Will you grant my wish tonight?
Let my little horse forlorn
Be at last a unicorn!

With a bright purple flash, Twilight stood before her in his unicorn form.

'Well, what do you think?' Lauren asked again.

'I need to see her before I can tell,' Twilight replied.

'OK, let's fly over there now,' Lauren said. She looked up at the dusky sky. 'It's dark enough and Mum and Dad won't miss me. Mum's busy working and Dad's watching a film on TV.'

She scrambled on to Twilight's back and, with a snort, he jumped up into the sky. He cantered towards the sliver of moon that had started to shine above the trees.

'Which way is it?' Twilight asked.

'Just out of town, to the north,' Lauren said, her hair blowing back from her face. 'It should be really quick to fly there. The roads took us a very twisty way round.'

She was right. Flying direct, they

reached High Meadows farm in five
minutes.

Lauren scanned the ground. The only
things moving seemed to be ponies. Tina
and her helpers had probably gone home
for the night.

'I think we can go down,' she said to
Twilight. 'It's that field over there by the
training ring. Look, there she is – the
little grey standing all by herself.'

As Twilight swooped down, the
palomino, bay and black ponies scattered
to the far side of the field with snorts of
alarm. But Moonshine didn't move. She
stared at Twilight as if transfixed. Her dark
eyes grew wider and then she lifted her
head and arched her neck. Shaking back

her mane, Moonshine stepped towards
Twilight, her delicate ears pricked, her
hooves moving daintily on the grass. She
looked so graceful with the moonlight
shining on her pale coat that Lauren
didn't need Twilight to tell her what he
thought. Moonshine *was* a unicorn. She
knew it beyond doubt.

Twilight whinnied softly. Moonshine
whickered back and as she reached him,
they extended their heads and touched
noses.

'Unicorn,' Lauren heard Twilight
murmur.

Moonshine snorted and looked at
Lauren.

'What's she saying?' Lauren asked.

'She's saying you told her that you had a unicorn,' Twilight translated. Moonshine whimpered sadly.

'She has never found anyone to be her Unicorn Friend,' Twilight said. 'It's all she's ever dreamed of.'

Lauren felt desperately sorry for the little pony. She knew that for a unicorn to be freed from its pony form, it needed to find a special person – a special person who believed in magic. Then they could share magical adventures together. 'Please tell her she will find someone to be her Unicorn Friend,' Lauren urged. She reached forward and patted Moonshine. 'You'll find someone who believes in magic. I know it.'

Lauren spoke determinedly but inside
she was far from sure. *I hope I'm right,* she
thought.

Moonshine bowed her head and
snorted quietly.

'She says she doesn't think it will
happen,' Twilight said softly.

Looking at the dejected little pony,
Lauren wanted to help her more than
anything else in the world. Sliding off
Twilight's back, she went over and
stroked Moonshine's neck to comfort
her. Moonshine looked up at her, her
dark eyes like deep forest pools.

Suddenly there was a change in her.
Moonshine's ears pricked and she
stiffened. She glanced round to the gate

and then, turning back to Twilight, she snorted anxiously.

Lauren saw a look of alarm cross Twilight's face.

'Quick, Lauren,' he said. 'There's someone coming!'

CHAPTER

Three

'Over there!' Lauren said, pointing
to a nearby copse.

Lauren swiftly mounted and Twilight
galloped among the trees. They were only
just in time. As they reached the shadows,
they saw a boy walk up to the gate and
climb over it. Lauren and Twilight waited
in the trees, watching without being seen.

The boy headed towards Moonshine.

He was skinny with untidy dark hair. He wasn't very tall but, judging by his face, Lauren guessed that he was probably about her age.

'Here, Moonshine,' she heard him say. He held out a handful of carrots. 'Here, beauty.'

Moonshine walked over to the boy. He fed her the carrots and stroked her tangled mane. 'Did you think I wasn't coming?'

Moonshine snorted.

Lauren bent low on Twilight's neck. 'Who is he?' she whispered. 'Did Moonshine say?'

'She doesn't know,' Twilight replied. 'She told me he started coming a few days ago – he's here for the summer with his family. He always brings her something to eat and just spends time talking to her and stroking her. Moonshine likes him.'

Lauren watched the boy talking softly to Moonshine and suddenly made a decision. 'Wait here,' she said to Twilight as she dismounted and walked out of the trees.

The boy almost jumped out of his skin. He stared at her in surprise and then turned and began to run down the field.

'Please, wait!' Lauren called, chasing after him.

But the boy didn't stop. He raced to the gate.

'Wait!' Lauren implored him, panting for breath as she ran after him. 'I only want to talk to you!'

Glancing over his shoulder, the boy tripped over a tree root and fell. It gave Lauren the time she needed to catch up with him. She grabbed his arm.

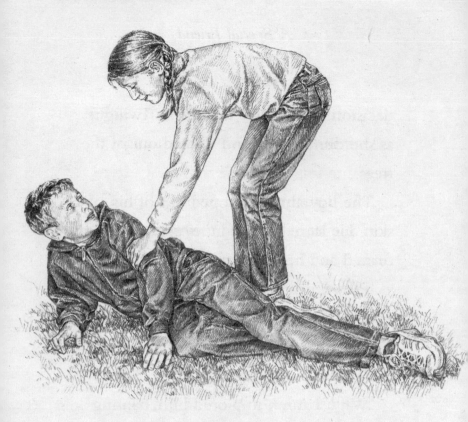

'I wasn't doing anything!' he gasped,
his face pale, his brown shock of hair
sticking up. 'I was just talking to the
pony. I wasn't hurting her, I promise.'

'I know you weren't,' Lauren said. 'It's
OK.'

The boy stared at her properly for the first time. 'You're ... you're not angry with me for feeding her?'

'No,' Lauren said in surprise. 'Of course not.' She let him go and they both stood up.

'Is it your pony?' he asked.

Lauren shook her head. 'No. She belongs to Tina, the woman who owns these stables.' She frowned. 'Who are you? What are you doing here?'

'My name's Michael,' the boy said warily. 'If Moonshine's not your pony, what are *you* doing in the field?'

Lauren didn't know what to reply. 'I ... er ... I was here today,' she said, 'with some friends who are buying a pony. I saw Moonshine and liked her.

I thought I'd come back and visit.' At
least it was half the truth.

Michael relaxed and, for the first time,
he smiled at her. 'That's why I'm here
too,' he confessed. 'I was exploring a few
days ago and I saw Moonshine in the
field. I thought she looked kind of lonely
so I started to visit her. I've been coming
every day. So, where do you live?'
Michael asked out of curiosity.

'Not too far away,' Lauren said vaguely,
thinking: *if you fly here*. 'How about you?'
she asked, changing the subject.

'Me?' Michael hesitated for a moment.
'In Washington,' he replied. 'Only I'm
staying in a house nearby for the summer
with my mum and dad. We've done a

house swap with a colleague of Jodie's ...
I mean my mum's.' He glanced at her,
wondering whether to say more. 'Jodie's
my adopted mum,' Michael explained
after a pause. 'I haven't been with them
long. My real mum died two years ago
and I was put into foster care.'

Lauren didn't know what to say. 'I'm
really sorry,' she stammered.

Michael gazed down. 'It's OK.'

He looked up and smiled as
Moonshine walked over to him, her
hooves echoing softly on the grass.

Moonshine snorted softly and rubbed
her head against Michael's chest. He
scratched her ears. There was silence for a
moment.

'It must be strange moving to the country just for the summer,' Lauren said sympathetically.

'Yes, it is,' Michael admitted. 'It's hard to fit in and make new friends when everyone's already settled.' He tried to look cheerful. 'But at least I get to see horses – you don't see many of them in the city.' He stroked Moonshine's face. 'I really wish I could have a pony of my own. I stayed on a farm for a while when I was being fostered. The people there taught me to ride. I love horses.'

'Me too,' Lauren said. 'Moonshine's for sale, you know,' she added carefully. She knew she'd only just met Michael but she was already beginning to think that he might make a good Unicorn Friend.

'For sale?' Michael echoed. His face lit up briefly then faded. 'Jodie and Chris – Mum and Dad – would never buy her for me.'

'Well, ponies are expensive to buy and look after,' Lauren agreed.

Michael shook his head. 'Oh, it's not the money. It's just they're not horsey people. When I started living with them I asked if I could go to a riding school, but they didn't take me seriously. They said that I would get bored and offered to buy me a bike and a skateboard instead.'

Michael looked sadly at Moonshine. 'Jodie and Chris are really nice, but they don't understand me at all . . .' He broke off, as if he'd said too much. 'Look, I'd better go,' he muttered. 'I'll see you.'

'I'm Lauren,' Lauren said, realizing she hadn't told him her name.

'See you, Lauren,' Michael said and immediately set off at a run.

'Wait! Where do you live?' Lauren called after him.

But Michael didn't stop. Climbing over the gate, he disappeared into the darkness. Lauren stared after him until she heard a familiar whicker.

Looking round, she saw Twilight walking out from the cover of the trees. It was clear from his expression that he had heard everything.

'Michael doesn't sound very happy,' he said, joining Lauren and Moonshine.

Lauren shook her head. 'No. It must be difficult having to get used to new parents and not knowing anyone round here.'

'Apart from Moonshine,' Twilight said, nuzzling the grey pony, who nuzzled him back before staring wistfully after

Michael. She whickered softly.

'Moonshine says she really likes him,' Twilight said. 'He's kind and gentle.'

'And lonely,' Lauren said. She sighed and looked at the little grey pony. Both Moonshine and Michael were so unhappy. She wished she and Twilight could help. But what could they do?

CHAPTER

Four

The following morning, Lauren had just finished her breakfast when Mr Parker arrived. As she got into the back of his car, it was obvious that Jessica and Samantha hadn't come to an agreement on which pony they should have. They were sitting, their arms crossed, arguing with each other.

'We're getting Bullfinch,' Samantha

was saying.

Jessica frowned. 'No, Sandy.'

'That's enough, you two,' Mr Parker warned. 'The idea of buying a pony was that you would have something to enjoy together, not to spend your time fighting over. If you're going to quarrel, we can just forget this pony idea completely.'

Jessica and Samantha quickly stopped arguing.

There was silence for a few minutes and then Jessica looked at her sister. 'Please, Samantha,' she said quietly, 'please can we get Sandy? You heard what Tina said yesterday – she's only six, she'll learn to jump better as she gets older. And I really, really like her.'

Samantha didn't say anything.

'We could have lessons on her, couldn't we, Dad?' Jessica asked.

Mr Parker nodded. 'Definitely – in fact, I think that would be a very good idea.'

'Then I guess she would improve, and she is pretty,' Samantha admitted. She frowned. 'OK, Jess, I'll think about it.'

Jessica exchanged hopeful looks with Lauren and they travelled the rest of the way in silence.

Lauren stared out of the window. She couldn't stop thinking about Michael. She wished she knew where he lived. If she did, she could call round with Twilight. Maybe they could fly back to Moonshine's field that night and see if he visited again.

When they arrived at the High Meadows farm, they saw that Tina was lunging Sandy in the training ring. The pony's golden coat gleamed in the sunlight and her thick, creamy-white tail floated out behind her. Her neck was arched and her dainty ears were pricked.

'Look, Sam!' Jessica exclaimed. 'Look how beautiful Sandy looks.'

Mr Parker stopped the car. Samantha, Jessica and Lauren jumped out and went over to the fence.

Seeing them, Tina waved. 'Hi, there,' she called, bringing the pony to a halt. 'Do you want to try Sandy and Bullfinch again?'

Jessica and Lauren looked at Samantha.

'Can we just try Sandy, please?' Samantha said to Tina.

★

Samantha and Jessica took it in turns to ride Sandy. She was lively but obedient and she jumped perfectly. By the time they had finished, Samantha was smiling.

'I like her,' she said, riding the pony over to the gate and halting her. 'She's been much better today.'

'And she'll continue to improve,' Tina said. 'You'll be able to do a lot with her.'

Jess turned to her dad. 'Can we have her, Dad? Please!'

'If it's all right with Sam then, OK!' Mr Parker smiled.

'Oh, thank you!' Jessica gasped. She turned to Samantha. 'And thank you for agreeing.'

'That's OK,' Samantha said happily. 'I really like her too, now I've ridden her again.'

While the girls put Sandy back in her stall, Mr Parker sorted out a price with Tina. It was arranged that she would deliver Sandy the next day.

'I can't believe she's going to be ours,' Jessica said as they got into the car.

'She's lovely,' Samantha said, looking genuinely pleased.

Mr Parker smiled. 'Well, I'm glad you two are in agreement at last. Come on, let's go home.'

As they turned out of the stables on to the quiet country road, something caught Lauren's eye. A boy with untidy dark hair

was riding a bike up and down the drive
of a nearby house. It was Michael! That
must be where he was staying with his
family!

She turned in her seat. Michael was
cycling in circles, looking bored.

'What are you looking at?' Jessica asked, following her gaze.

'Nothing,' Lauren said quickly.

To her relief, Jessica didn't press any more. She squeezed Lauren's arm. 'It's brilliant that Samantha and I are going to keep Sandy at Mel's, isn't it? We'll be able to ride together every day.'

'Yeah, it'll be great,' Lauren agreed. Mel Cassidy was one of their friends. She lived on the farm next door to Lauren but she was away at summer camp at the moment. Jessica started to talk about everything they would do together when Mel got back. Lauren listened vaguely but her thoughts were on Michael. Now she knew where he

lived maybe she could ride over on
Twilight to visit him. It wouldn't be that
far if they went through the woods
instead of going round by the roads.
Michael could have a ride on Twilight.
Determination filled Lauren. She was
going to help him. She was going to be
his friend.

It took Lauren and Twilight just over half
an hour to reach Michael's house through
the woods. A narrow track brought them
out on to the road beside his house.

As they rode along it, Lauren heard a
woman's voice coming from the garden.
'What would you like to do, Michael? We
could go swimming?'

There was no reply.

'Well, how about we go to the park?' Lauren heard the woman say.

'Yeah, I guess,' Michael replied quietly. Suddenly he spoke again. 'There's a pony! I can hear a pony coming!'

He came running down the drive. Recognizing Lauren, his eyes widened.

Lauren waved. 'Hi!'

'It's ... it's you!' Michael stammered in surprise.

Lauren grinned. 'Yes, and this is my pony, Twilight. Do you like him?'

Michael nodded, looking astonished. 'I didn't know you had a pony.'

'You left last night before I could tell you,' Lauren explained.

'He looks just like Moonshine,' Michael said.

Just then, a slim woman in her thirties with short dark hair came down the drive. She wore a pretty lilac sundress with matching sandals. This must be Jodie, Michael's foster mum. 'Who are you talking to, Michael?' She stopped in surprise when she saw Twilight and Lauren.

'My name's Lauren Foster,' Lauren said in her politest voice. 'I met Michael yesterday —'

'When I went out for a walk,' Michael put in quickly.

'I thought I'd call round and say hi,' Lauren said. 'I hope you don't mind.'

'No, no, of course not,' Jodie said quickly.

'Michael told me he liked horses and I thought he might like a ride on my pony, Twilight,' Lauren said. 'We could ride in the woods.' She looked at Michael. 'If you bring your bike we could take it in turns to ride Twilight.'

Michael's face lit up. 'Great!' He turned to Jodie. 'I can, can't I?'

Jodie looked unsure. 'Well, are you sure you want to, honey?'

'Yes!' Michael exclaimed. 'Please can I?'

Jodie looked taken aback. 'Well, I guess so.' She glanced rather dubiously at Twilight. 'He is safe, isn't he?'

'Very,' Lauren said. 'And Michael can wear my hat.'

'Well, OK then,' Jodie said. 'But don't be out too long.'

'Let's go into the woods,' Lauren said

as Michael pushed his bike down the drive to join her.

'This is fantastic!' Michael said, looking incredibly happy. 'How did you know where we were staying?'

Lauren explained about visiting the stables with Jessica's family. 'I saw you and thought I'd come round and visit.'

They reached the main trail. Lauren stopped Twilight and dismounted. 'Here, you have a go,' she said, handing her hat to Michael.

He put it on and mounted. 'Wow!' he said, beaming. 'It's amazing to be on a pony again.'

'You can trot and canter if you like,' Lauren said. 'Twilight's very good.'

To start with, Michael just walked, but as his confidence grew he trotted and cantered. He wasn't a very experienced rider, but his hands were light on the reins and he had very good balance. At last he reined Twilight in. His eyes were shining and his cheeks were flushed. 'That was brilliant! Twilight's fantastic, Lauren!'

Lauren smiled. 'I know. I'm really lucky.'

They rode for a while longer before Michael glanced at his watch. 'I guess I should be getting back.'

They headed to his house. Jodie was standing on the front porch looking out

for them. 'There you are,' she said,
coming down the steps towards them. 'I
was starting to worry.'

Michael looked at the ground. 'Sorry,'
he mumbled.

'It's OK,' Jodie said quickly. 'You must
be hungry after your ride. Would you like
some cookies? I baked them this morning.'

'Yes, please,' Lauren said.

Michael just nodded.

Lauren looked at him in surprise. He
had been chatty out in the woods but
now he was quiet. Jodie went inside.

'Your new mum seems really nice,'
Lauren said in a low voice as she tied
Twilight up to the fence at the side of
the house.

'She is,' Michael said. There was a
flatness in his voice. 'Both she and Chris
are.' He sat down on the porch steps.

Lauren heard a note of reservation in
his voice. 'But . . . ?' she asked, sitting
down beside him.

For a moment Michael seemed to be
wondering whether to say anything
more. 'But they like different things from
me,' he said, with a sigh. 'And that makes
it hard.'

'What do you mean?' Lauren asked
curiously.

'Well, Chris is really into baseball,'
Michael replied, 'and he's always
suggesting we go out and practise. And
Jodie's always trying to get me to go

swimming. I want to please them so I just go along with them, but really I just want to be with horses.'

'What do they say when you ask if you can go riding?' Lauren said.

Michael shrugged. 'I don't really ask. I did once or twice at the beginning but not any more.'

'Why not?' Lauren demanded in surprise.

'I want to make them happy,' Michael said softly. 'I want them to be glad they adopted me ...'

He broke off as Jodie came out of the house with a tray of drinks and chocolate-chip cookies.

'Here we are,' she said cheerfully,

putting the tray down on a table on the
porch. 'Have a cookie, Lauren.'

'Thank you,' Lauren said.

Jodie smiled. 'You know, I'm really pleased Michael's made a friend,' she said, sitting down on the steps too. 'What sort of things do you and your friends do in the holidays, Lauren?'

'We go to the creek and we go round to each other's houses, but most of all we ride,' Lauren said. 'Most of my friends have ponies.'

Jodie frowned. 'Really? Goodness. Things are different in the country. I grew up in the city. None of my friends ever rode.'

'Maybe Michael could start to ride while you're here,' Lauren suggested hopefully.

'Oh, I'm not sure,' Jodie said

doubtfully. 'You'd probably find it a bit boring, wouldn't you, Michael?'

'No!' Michael said, looking up quickly. 'I'd love to go riding.'

Lauren's eyes suddenly widened. She'd just had a brilliant idea!

Five

'There are stables just round the corner from here,' Lauren burst out, looking at Jodie. 'Maybe Michael could help out there for the summer. He'd get to know people and he could be with horses.'

'That would be amazing!' Michael gasped. 'Can I?' he begged Jodie. 'Can I, please?'

Jodie raised her eyebrows. 'You wouldn't really want to, would you?'

'Yes,' Michael said. 'I'd love to.'

'Well, I suppose I *could* speak to the owner,' Jodie said.

Michael jumped up. 'Now?' he asked eagerly.

Jodie looked at him in amazement. 'You *are* keen. Well, OK. If it means that much to you then we can go and ask right away.' She finished her drink. 'I'll just lock the house and get my bag.'

Tina was leading Puzzle in from the field when Lauren arrived with Michael and Jodie. Jodie explained what they had come round for.

'Michael likes the idea of helping out,' she said to Tina. 'Do you let children do that?'

'Yes,' Tina replied. 'I usually have at least five or six of them helping me in exchange for rides. At the moment several are away at camp. I could do with another pair of hands.' She looked at Michael. 'The trouble is, you're younger than most of my helpers and I won't be able to offer you many rides. I think a lot of the ponies will be too strong for you.'

'That's OK,' Michael said quickly. 'I'd be happy just to help.'

Twilight suddenly lifted his head and neighed. From the field by the car park came an answering whinny. Tina looked round. Moonshine was standing at the gate, staring at them.

She scratched her head. 'I suppose there's always Moonshine,' she said. 'She's very quiet. You could ride her, Michael.'

'I'd love to!' Michael said. He looked at Lauren, his eyes shining.

'OK then,' Tina said. 'It's settled. You come and help me with the yard chores and you can ride Moonshine in exchange.'

'And can I groom her and clean her tack?' Michael asked eagerly.

Tina smiled at his enthusiasm. 'As much as you like.'

Lauren was desperate to talk to Twilight about the good news. She couldn't wait until that evening and so on the way

home, she turned him down an
overgrown path that led to a hidden
glade in the woods.

Twilight walked forward eagerly,
pushing his way through the overhanging
branches. At last, the path opened out
into the sunny clearing. The grass was
springy and scattered with purple flowers.
Golden butterflies fluttered through the
warm, sweet-scented air. It was the most
secret place Lauren knew.

She said the Turning Spell.

'So, what do you think?' she asked, as
soon as the purple flash faded and
Twilight was standing in front of her in
his unicorn form.

'It's a wonderful idea,' Twilight said.

'Moonshine will love having someone to look after her each day.'

'And Michael will love helping with all the ponies,' Lauren said.

Twilight nodded. 'He would make a very good Unicorn Friend.'

'I know,' Lauren agreed. 'But I guess Moonshine's just going to have to wait for someone else to come along. Michael's only here for another five weeks, so he probably won't have time to find out that she's a unicorn.'

'Unless we help him,' Twilight said thoughtfully.

Lauren frowned. 'But we can't, Twilight. You know Unicorn Friends have to find out the truth about their

unicorn by themselves. That's why Mrs
Fontana could only hint that you were a
unicorn when I got you. We can't tell
Michael. If he's going to be a Unicorn
Friend, he has to believe in magic
enough to try the spell without knowing
whether it will work.'

Twilight nodded. 'I know, and I didn't
mean that we should tell him everything,
but couldn't we sort of *help* him find out
the truth?'

'I guess so,' Lauren said slowly. A
thought struck her. 'But if he does find
out, what will happen when he has to
leave Moonshine at the end of the
summer? It will be awful for him.'

'But isn't it better he has five weeks

as a Unicorn Friend than none?'
Twilight pointed out.

Lauren hesitated. She wasn't sure. It
was going to be hard enough for Michael
to leave Moonshine at the end of the
summer. Surely it would be a hundred
times worse if he had to leave her
knowing she was a unicorn?

'I don't know,' she said uncertainly. She
twisted her fingers in Twilight's mane and
wondered how she would feel if she had
to leave Twilight. *I couldn't bear it,* she
thought.

But what if she had never known
about his unicorn powers? Not known
what it was like to fly through the starry
skies, to feel the wind against her face

and Twilight's warm back beneath her?
Not even having the memories … No,
that would be even worse.

Twilight nuzzled her. 'What does your
heart say, Lauren?'

Lauren hesitated. Yes, it would be
dreadful for Michael to have to leave
Moonshine at the end of the summer
but, like Twilight had said, surely it was
better that he did that instead of never
knowing the truth. 'My heart says that we
should help him,' she said slowly.

'Well, I think that too,' Twilight said.
'So let's do it!'

Lauren looked at him. His dark eyes
were eager. She paused and then made a
decision.

'OK,' she agreed.

As she spoke, she felt a weight drop off her shoulders. She was sure that they were doing the right thing. They should help Michael. The only question was, *how were they going to do it*?

Even though Lauren thought about it all night, by the time she rode Twilight to Tina's the next morning she hadn't come up with an answer. Michael was riding Moonshine in the ring when she arrived. Moonshine was cantering eagerly, her ears pricked.

Michael saw them. 'Hi there,' he called.

'Moonshine's looking good,' Lauren said.

Michael bent down and hugged Moonshine's neck. 'She's brilliant.'

Tina came up the yard. Seeing Lauren, she smiled. 'Hello. Come to visit?'

Lauren nodded. 'You don't mind, do you?'

'Not at all,' Tina said. She looked at Michael. 'That's probably enough ring-work for Moonshine today. Why don't you go out into the woods for a short ride?'

'OK,' Michael said eagerly.

He rode out of the yard with Lauren. 'So, are you enjoying helping Tina?' she asked.

'It's brilliant,' Michael said, his face glowing. 'I've mucked out five stables

already this morning. This is going to be
the best holiday ever.'

Lauren stroked Twilight. Michael's
holiday would be even better if he knew
about Moonshine. But how could she
help him? She couldn't just start talking
about unicorns out of the blue, he'd
think she was crazy.

Beside her, Michael patted
Moonshine's neck. 'You know, I'm sure
Moonshine understands me when I talk
to her,' he said. 'It's the way she looks at
me. Like she's smarter than other ponies.'
He laughed, sounding suddenly
embarrassed. 'I guess that sounds really
dumb.'

'No, it doesn't,' Lauren said. 'I know

what you mean. Twilight's the same. It's like they're different from other ponies.'

She glanced quickly at Michael. Maybe this was her chance to say something more. But what could she say? Before she could think of anything, Michael had pushed Moonshine on.

'Come on, let's canter!' he called.

Twilight jumped forward eagerly.

Lauren had no choice but to let him race after the little grey mare. She felt a wave of frustration at the wasted chance. Michael would be a perfect Unicorn Friend if only he would try the spell. But how did she get him to do that? Maybe if she had lots of time she could think of a way, but in just five weeks Michael would be going back to the city.

I'll come up with something, Lauren thought, crouching low against Twilight's neck as he cantered along the path. *I just have to.*

CHAPTER

Six

A week passed by but Lauren didn't get any further in helping Michael work out Moonshine's secret. It was so frustrating. The more she saw him with Moonshine, and realized how much he loved the pony, the more she wanted him to be Moonshine's Unicorn Friend. But she just couldn't think of how to help him find out the truth. It just seemed impossible.

On Saturday, Michael came round to
her house and they went down to the
creek with Jessica and Samantha. They
took it in turns to ride Twilight and
Sandy. When they got back to her house
they brushed Twilight down and then
went up to Lauren's bedroom.

'I like your room,' Michael said,
looking admiringly at the horse posters
Lauren had stuck on the walls. He went
over to the window. 'Hey, you can see
Twilight's paddock from here.' Lauren's
unicorn book was lying open on the
window seat. Michael picked it up and
started to leaf through the pages. 'Wow!
This book looks interesting.'

Lauren's heart leapt. Of course! The

book had all the information Michael
needed.

Michael turned the first page. 'Look at

this pony! It looks just like Twilight and Moonshine.'

'It's a picture of what unicorns look like when they're disguised,' Lauren said.

'What do you mean?' Michael asked looking round at her.

And suddenly Lauren knew as clearly as anything what she had to do. 'Read the book and it'll tell you,' she told him. 'You can borrow it for the holidays.'

Michael looked surprised. 'Are you sure?'

Lauren nodded. She loved the book and didn't want to let it go – even for a few weeks – but she was sure that it was the only way that Michael was going to learn about unicorns.

'OK, thanks,' he said, looking really pleased.

'Lauren!' Mrs Foster called up the stairs. 'Michael's mum is here.'

'We'd better go,' Lauren said. They went downstairs. Jodie was in the kitchen.

'Hi, honey,' she said, as Michael came in. 'Have you had a good day?'

Michael's eyes shone. 'It's been great! We rode to the creek with Lauren's friends, Jessica and Samantha, and we had a picnic and we swam.'

'That sounds fun,' Jodie said.

'It was fantastic!' Michael said. He looked round. 'I left my bag in your tack room, Lauren. Can I go and get it?'

'Sure,' Lauren said.

Michael put the unicorn book down on the table and ran outside. Jodie shook her head. 'I just can't believe the change in him since we moved out to the country for the summer,' she said to Mrs Foster. 'He used to be so quiet, but now he talks all the time – although only about horses.'

Mrs Foster laughed. 'That sounds very familiar. Is he going to carry on riding when you return to the city?'

'We'll see,' Jodie replied. 'Kids in the city don't really ride.'

Lauren looked at her mum. 'I used to ride lots when we lived in the city, didn't I, Mum?'

Mrs Foster nodded. 'We only moved here at Easter,' she explained to Jodie. 'Before then, Lauren used to ride every weekend. I know it's not so easy but there are riding schools and kids who ride. It's a good hobby, the children learn responsibility and have fun at the same time.'

Jodie looked surprised. 'Oh, I see.'

Michael came back in. 'I've got it,' he said, waving his bag. He started to put the book carefully inside. 'Thanks for having me round, Mrs Foster.'

'It's a pleasure,' Mrs Foster replied.

'What have you got there?' Jodie asked Michael, looking at the book.

'Lauren's lent it to me,' Michael

answered. 'It's a book about unicorns.'

Lauren sensed her mum glance quickly at her. Her mum knew that the unicorn book was one of the most precious things Lauren owned.

'Well, thank you very much, Lauren,' Jodie said.

'I'm sure Michael will take very good
care of it.'

Lauren nodded and she and her mum
saw Jodie and Michael to their car.

'So?' her mum said quietly to her as
they waved them off.

'So?' Lauren said, but she knew what
her mum was getting at.

'The book,' Mrs Foster said, looking at
her. 'You love that book, Lauren. I'm
surprised you're letting it out of your
sight.'

'I know,' Lauren said. 'But Michael was
looking at it today and he really liked it
and . . .' she hesitated, 'and I wanted to
lend it to him for the summer.'

Her mum looked at her for a moment.

Then she smiled. 'There's a lot of good in you, Lauren Foster,' she said, hugging her. 'I'm proud you're my daughter.' She kissed Lauren's hair.

'Mum!' Lauren protested, but she felt a warm glow inside.

They walked back into the house.

'Michael really does love ponies, doesn't he?' Mrs Foster said. 'I guess it must be strange for his parents if they've never been into horses themselves and don't know anyone who rides. It probably seems an odd thing for him to want to do. Still, maybe if they see how much he enjoys himself this summer they'll let him carry on riding when they go home.'

Lauren nodded. But she couldn't really think about Michael going back to the city. Right now all that mattered was him finding out Moonshine's secret. Would he read the book? And, even more important, would he believe it? Lauren crossed her fingers. She and Twilight were just going to have to wait and see.

As Lauren rode Twilight over to High Meadows farm early the next morning, she said, 'I wonder if Michael read the book last night.' A thought struck her. 'What if he doesn't believe it? I had the book for ages before I tried turning you into a unicorn, Twilight.' She thought back to that time. 'It was only when I

saw the moonflowers in the secret glade
that I started to wonder if the spell might
actually work,' she said.

Twilight stopped dead.

'What's wrong?' Lauren said.

To her surprise, Twilight turned round
and started heading back down the track.
'What are you doing?' Lauren asked in
astonishment.

Twilight broke into a trot. Lauren
quickly loosened the reins. It was clear
he'd had an idea about something,
although she didn't know what. She let
him go where he wanted.

He trotted for about two minutes down
the path, finally halting by the overgrown
trail that led to the secret glade.

'Why have you stopped here?' Lauren said.

Twilight started to walk down the trail. Lauren ducked under the branches, wondering what he was doing. As soon as they entered the glade, he plunged his head down to the ground.

'You came here because you wanted to eat some grass?' Lauren said in surprise. Twilight stamped his hoof and she suddenly realized that he wasn't eating. He was nudging a moonflower with his nose.

Her eyes widened as she finally understood. 'You think we should take a moonflower to Michael?'

Twilight nodded.

'It's a brilliant idea!' Lauren said. 'He probably just thinks they're made-up flowers in the book, but if I give one to him he'll see that they really exist and maybe it'll make him try the spell.' She jumped off and picked a flower.

Twilight tossed his head as if to say, *That's what I thought all along.* Putting the flower in her pocket, Lauren remounted and they carried on their way.

Moonshine was tied up in the yard at High Meadows farm. Lauren noticed how much better she was looking. Her coat was now sleek and grey and her mane and tail were silky.

Michael came out of a barn with a

wheelbarrow. He was
deep in thought.

'Hi,' Lauren called.

Michael looked up. 'Oh . . . hi.'

'Are you free to go for a ride?' Lauren
asked.

'I've got another two stalls to muck
out first,' Michael said. 'But then I can.'

Lauren dismounted. 'I'll give you a
hand.' She tied Twilight up by Moonshine
and then set to work, watching Michael
carefully all the time.

For a while Michael worked in silence,
but at last he spoke. 'I was reading that
book last night.'

Lauren glanced at him eagerly. 'What
did you think?'

'It was really good.' He laughed in an
embarrassed way. 'I mean, I know it's not
true or anything but it's a really good
story.'

Lauren remembered the flower. It was
now or never. 'I brought you something

from the woods.' She took the
moonflower out of her jeans. The gold
spots on the tip of each purple petal
seemed to glow in the light of the stall.

Michael looked as if he was wondering
why she had brought him a flower but
then his eyes widened. 'It's a ... it's a ...'

'Moonflower,' Lauren murmured.

Michael's eyes flew to hers. 'They really exist?'

Lauren nodded. 'Yes, and so does the Twilight Star. It shines every night for ten minutes just after the sun sets.' She met his eyes. 'You just have to believe.'

Michael stared.

Fearing that, in a minute, she'd tell him everything, Lauren pushed the flower into his hand. 'Here, take it. I'll empty the wheelbarrow.' Before he could ask her any questions, she grabbed the handles of the wheelbarrow and pushed it out of the stall.

Michael didn't say much for the rest of the morning. He seemed to be thinking hard and even when they went out on a ride, he remained quiet. On the way home, Lauren caught him looking from Moonshine to Twilight. *Oh, please*, she thought, *try the spell tonight*.

They got back to the yard to find Jodie coming out of the office with Tina.

Seeing the surprise on Michael's face, Jodie smiled. 'Don't worry, nothing's wrong. I just thought I'd call round and see Tina and find out how you were doing.'

'And I said you were doing great,' Tina said. 'Moonshine's been like a different pony since you started looking after her, Michael.'

'So, this is Moonshine, is it?' Jodie asked, looking interested.

'Yes,' Michael answered. 'Isn't she perfect?'

Jodie stroked Moonshine. 'Oh, she is pretty.'

'She's the best,' Michael said, leaning forward and hugging the little grey pony. 'Aren't you, girl? She understands everything.'

Lauren patted Twilight's neck. If only Michael knew how true that was ...

CHAPTER
Seven

The next morning, Lauren was up
and out of the house by nine
o'clock. She was longing to see Michael.

Michael was grooming Moonshine
when Lauren rode into the yard at High
Meadows farm. The little pony's coat
looked even glossier and her dark eyes
had a new sparkle.

'Hi,' Lauren called eagerly.

Michael swung round. 'Hello!' The
word almost burst out of him. He looked
very excited. 'Lauren!' he said, running
over. 'I've got to tell you something!
Something amazing about Moonshine.
She's a –'

'Ssshh,' Lauren interrupted, quickly
dismounting. 'I know.'

Michael stared at her. 'What do you
mean, you know?'

Lauren looked pointedly at Twilight.
He followed her gaze and his eyes
widened. 'Twilight's a –'

'You mustn't tell anyone,' Lauren broke
in. 'No one must know about him or
Moonshine. You can't talk about it – not
to anyone. It's got to be a secret.'

'But ... but ...' Michael stammered.

'Remember what the book said,'
Lauren reminded him.

They stared at each other for a
moment.

'I can't believe it's true,' Michael said,
shaking his head in wonder.

Lauren smiled. 'It is. Believe me, it is.'

Just then, Tina came out of the barn. She was showing a man and a dark-haired girl around the yard.

Lauren stiffened. 'I know that girl. She's called Monica Corder. She's in my class at school. What's she doing here?'

Michael looked surprised. 'She and her dad are looking for a pony, I think.'

'She's not very nice,' Lauren said.

'There's nothing here,' Monica was saying loudly to her dad. 'I want a pony that's going to win things.'

'Well, how about that chestnut with the blaze?' Mr Corder said. He turned to Tina. 'You said he'd won a lot lately.'

Monica folded her arms. 'But I don't want a chestnut, I want a grey.'

'Why don't you just give him a try, Monica?' Mr Corder said.

'I guess I could,' Monica said grudgingly.

'Michael,' Tina called. 'Can you tack up Puzzle for me, please?'

Monica glanced in their direction. Seeing Lauren, she frowned in surprise. 'Lauren! What are you doing here?' she said, speaking as if Lauren had no right to be in Tina's yard. Before Lauren could reply, Monica's eyes had fallen on Moonshine. 'Hey! What's *that* pony's name?' she demanded.

'Moonshine,' Michael replied.

Monica's green gaze swept over Moonshine's soft grey coat and silky mane and tail. 'I like her,' she declared. She turned to her father. 'Dad! I like this pony. She's really pretty. I'll try her too.'

Lauren and Michael stared at each other in horror.

Mr Corder turned to Tina. 'We'll have that one saddled up too, please.'

'Well, actually,' Tina said, stepping forward, 'I've already got someone booked to see that pony later this morning. They've asked to be given first refusal on her – that means they have first choice on whether to buy her or not,' she explained to Monica. 'So although you can try her out, I have to wait and let the other people see her as well.'

Lauren stared at Tina. There were other people who wanted Moonshine? But they couldn't. Moonshine couldn't be sold! Especially not now Michael had discovered her secret.

Monica scowled. 'But I like her best.'

'I'm sorry, but that's the situation,' Tina said.

'Well, I'll try her anyway,' Monica said.

Tina turned to Michael. 'Can you tack Moonshine up as well, please, Michael?'

Michael looked totally shocked as he fetched the tack. Lauren felt awful. Poor Michael. What would he do if Moonshine was sold?

★

Monica mounted Moonshine. She landed
with a thump in the saddle and
Moonshine took a surprised step
backwards.

'Walk on!' Monica said sharply, digging
her heels into Moonshine's sides. When

Moonshine didn't respond immediately,
Monica smacked her with her riding
crop. Moonshine jumped forward in
alarm. Lauren glanced at Michael. His
face was pale.

'Just give her time to get used to you,
Monica,' Tina called, standing by the gate
with Puzzle.

Monica dug her heels in again. 'Come
on.'

Moonshine's walk slowed down.
Monica smacked her again with her crop.
'Walk on!'

But Moonshine just got slower and
slower. Although she was very good for
Michael she seemed determined to be as
lazy as possible for Monica.

After a circuit of the ring, Monica stopped Moonshine by the gate. 'She's a useless pony,' she said scathingly. 'She's so slow.' She dismounted. 'She's way too lazy for me.'

Lauren felt a rush of relief.

'Oh well, never mind,' Tina said cheerfully. 'I think the people who are coming later this morning will be just perfect for her.'

Lauren glanced at her. Tina didn't sound like she cared about Michael's feelings. Surely she knew how upset he was at the thought of Moonshine being sold?

'I'll try the other pony instead,' Monica said.

As she mounted Puzzle, Tina turned to
Michael. 'Seeing as Moonshine's tacked
up, why don't you take her out for a
quick ride in the woods, Michael? The
other people won't be here for a while
and you can smarten her up when you
get back.'

Michael nodded. Lauren realized that
Tina had suggested the ride to be kind
because she could see that Michael was
only just managing to fight back his tears.

As they rode out of the yard, Lauren
looked at him. 'I'm really sorry,' she said.

Michael stared at Moonshine's mane.
'She can't be sold,' he said in a low
trembling voice.

'At least Monica didn't want her,'

Lauren said, trying to cheer him up. 'And maybe she'll be just as lazy for these other people, then they won't want her either.' She leaned forward. 'Moonshine. You've got to do exactly what you did with Monica this afternoon. These people *mustn't* buy you.'

Moonshine nodded slightly.

'And maybe we can put these people off her,' Lauren said, trying to think of something. 'Tell them that she's naughty or something.'

'Yes.' Michael looked suddenly hopeful, but then his face fell. 'I won't be here. Jodie and Chris are taking me shopping later.'

'Well, I'll stay,' Lauren said. 'I'll try and

think of something.'

Michael swallowed. 'I know I've got to
say to goodbye to Moonshine at the end
of the summer but not now, especially
not after finding out that she's a –'

'Ssshh!' Lauren said quickly in case
there was anyone nearby in the woods
who might overhear.

She saw a tear fall down Michael's
face. 'I'll think of something,' she said
desperately. 'I promise.'

CHAPTER

Eight

As Lauren and Michael rode back to
the yard, Tina came out of a barn.
'Great, you're back. Can you brush
Moonshine over and oil her hooves,
Michael?'

'Did Monica buy Puzzle?' Lauren
asked.

Tina shook her head. 'She didn't like
him, although at least he was better

behaved than Moonshine.' She walked
over and patted the little grey pony next
to Michael. 'I've never known you so
lazy, girl. I guess you just didn't like her.'

Leaving Michael to smarten up
Moonshine, Tina went to the tack room.
Lauren tried desperately to think of a
plan.

'I'm going to have to go in a minute,'
Michael said, looking at his watch after
he'd oiled Moonshine's hooves. 'Have you
thought of anything, Lauren?'

She shook her head. 'Not yet.'

'What am I going to do?' he said.

Just then there was the sound of a car
coming down the drive. Tina came out of
the tack room. 'Ah, here are the people to

see Moonshine.'

Michael and Lauren looked round at the black car.

'No it's not, Tina. It's my mum and dad,' Michael said. 'They must have decided to come and get me. We're going shopping.'

'Yes,' Tina said with a smile. 'I know.'

Lauren looked at her. There was something about the way she was smiling ...

Michael had obviously noticed it too. He looked from Tina to his mum and dad who were parking the car. 'What ... what's going on?' he asked.

'Yes, you're going shopping, Michael – for a pony,' Tina told him.

Both Lauren and Michael stared at her.

'A pony!' Michael gasped.

Tina nodded. 'When your mum came
to see me yesterday, it was to talk about
buying you Moonshine. I suggested she
come with your dad to see her today.'

'I . . . I don't believe it,'
Michael stammered. Jodie
and Chris got out of the car.
Jodie small and slim, Chris tall and skinny
with round glasses. Michael raced over to
them. 'I'm getting a pony? I'm really
getting Moonshine?' His eyes looked
almost wild.

'If you want her,' Jodie said.

'Oh yes, I do! More than anything!' Michael cried.

'Then she's yours,' Chris smiled.

'But where will I keep her?' Michael burst out.

'I phoned some stables in the city and found one near home,' Jodie said. 'They have a pony club there. You'll be able to learn all sorts of things – have lessons, go in shows.'

Chris nodded. 'And they run stable management classes for the parents too, so Jodie and I will be able to learn about horses and help you.' He squeezed Michael's shoulder. 'If you want us to, of course.'

Michael looked almost lost for words.

'That . . . that would be great.' He swung round. 'Lauren! Did you hear that?'

She grinned at him. 'Yes. It's great!'

Michael grabbed hold of Jodie and Chris's hands. 'Come and see Moonshine,' he said, half pulling them up the yard.

Moonshine whickered as they got close. Michael ran over and patted her proudly. 'You're going to be mine!' he told her.

'We just want you to be happy,' Jodie said to him, smiling at his joyful face. 'It's all we've ever wanted. We only tried to get you to do things like baseball and swimming because we thought you'd enjoy them.'

'I know,' Michael said. 'It's just that I like horses.'

'I guess we only realized that once we saw how much you've liked coming and helping here,' Chris said. 'I mean before that you'd only mentioned riding once or twice.'

'I know.' Michael looked awkward. 'It was because you didn't seem keen on the idea when I did mention it so I stopped. I wanted to please you and do what you wanted.'

'I think we've all been trying a bit too hard,' Jodie said. 'Maybe now the three of us can really start being a family.' She walked forward and patted the little grey pony. 'Sorry, I should have said the four

of us, of course. Welcome to the family,
Moonshine.'

Moonshine whickered softly and
Michael threw his arms round Jodie and
Chris in delight. They
hugged him
tightly.

Lauren's thoughts were whirling. She could hardly believe that after she and Michael had been so worried things had all ended perfectly.

Michael sighed happily and looked at Moonshine. 'You're going to be mine, Moonshine! I can't believe it!'

Tina smiled at him. 'I told you she'd be going to a perfect home, didn't I?'

Michael nodded. 'But I didn't know you meant me. I'm so lucky. She's the best pony in the world!'

Twilight snorted.

'One of the two best ponies in the world,' Michael corrected himself.

The adults laughed.

'Everyone thinks their pony is the best

pony in the world,' Tina commented.

Michael grinned at Lauren. 'But in our case it's true, isn't it?'

Lauren grinned back. 'Definitely,' she said.

The night air was warm and still as Lauren and Twilight stood in the shadow of the trees waiting for Michael to visit Moonshine. Twilight bent to rub his head against his knee as a shaft of moonlight shone down through the branches and glanced off his pearly horn.

'He's coming,' Lauren whispered. 'Look.'

Twilight lifted his head. Michael was hurrying down the drive.

Moonshine was waiting by the gate.
She whinnied softly, her ears pricked.
Michael climbed the gate and stood
beside her, his hand on her grey neck.

Lauren saw his lips move. Suddenly there was a bright purple flash and Moonshine was transformed into a unicorn. She was beautiful, her long tail swept almost to

the ground and her coat gleamed like
mother of pearl in the moonlight.

'What should we do?' Twilight
murmured. 'Do you think we should go
over and say hello?'

Lauren looked at Michael and
Moonshine. They were standing only
inches apart, their heads almost touching.
They looked lost in their own little
world.

'No,' Lauren said suddenly. 'Let's leave
them.'

As she spoke, Michael got on to
Moonshine's back. Moonshine turned
and, pushing off with her hind legs, she
cantered up into the sky. Lauren smiled,
her eyes shining. At long last Moonshine

had found a true Unicorn Friend and it
wasn't just for the summer. It looked like
they were going to be together for a

long, long time to come – just like her
and Twilight.

As she turned Twilight for home,
Lauren buried her face in his silvery
mane. They had so many more wonderful
adventures ahead of them – she couldn't
wait!

My Secret Unicorn

Most of the time, Twilight looks like an ordinary grey pony, but when Lauren says the words of a spell he transforms into a magical unicorn and together they can fly all over the world . . .

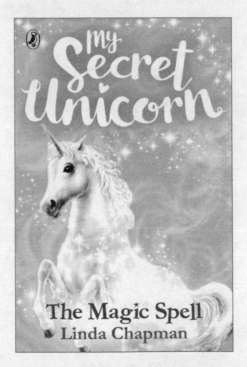

Look out for more *My Secret Unicorn* adventures

My Secret Unicorn

Lauren's nervous about starting a new school and making new friends. Can Twilight's magical powers help?

Look out for more *My Secret Unicorn* adventures

My Secret Unicorn

Lauren's friend Jessica is finding life at home difficult. Lauren and Twilight want to help her but can they persuade her to trust them?

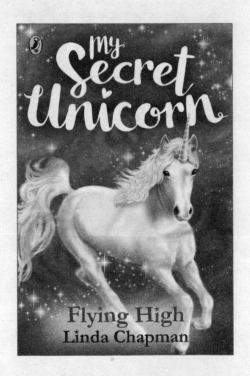

My Secret Unicorn

Flying High
Linda Chapman

Look out for more *My Secret Unicorn* adventures

Cover illustrations © Andrew Farley

My Secret Unicorn

There are rumours going round school that there is
a haunted treehouse by the creek. It's up to Lauren
and Twilight to solve the spooky mystery!

Look out for more *My Secret Unicorn* adventures

Cover illustrations © Andrew Farley

My Secret Unicorn

On one of their evening fly-arounds Twilight starts
to feel ill and he and Lauren have to stop exploring
and return home. Can they find something stronger
than magic to help Twilight get bettter. . .?

Look out for more *My Secret Unicorn* adventures

Cover illustrations © Andrew Farley